Frizzle's Funky Day at the ZOO

Happy Town Zoo & Gardens

Author and Illustrator
Rhonda Goodall

First SYP Publishing Edition
Frizzle's Funky Day at the Zoo
Library of Congress Control Number: 2020947445
ISBN-13: 978-1-59616-114-6
First Printing 2020
Published in the United States of America
Printed in the United States of America

Frizzle's Funky Day at the Zoo

Dedicated to families ... and the love that holds us all together.

Author and Illustrator
Rhonda Goodall

"For Patty.....
Who embraced and celebrated the uniqueness in all of us"

Frizzle's Funky Day at the ZOO

Frizzle is a, well,
he's a..., um,
well, just look at him.
He's a..., hmmm...,
you know, he's a Frizzle.

After feeling like it would never come, Frizzle was thrilled, because Saturday had finally arrived in Happy Town!!!

He had been waiting for weeks for this Saturday to get here!

Frizzle and Mr. Owl were going to the Zoo!

Happy Town
Zoo & Gardens

3.

Frizzle's Funky Day at the ZOO

Happy Town
Zoo & Gardens

They planned to meet at the
Happy Town Zoo and Gardens at one o'clock.

Neither Frizzle nor Mr. Owl
had been to the new Zoo yet.
It had just opened in the last couple months.

Because Frizzle was excited,
and he felt like the morning was dragging,
he decided to head to the Zoo early.

As Frizzle walked through the entrance gates,
he was mesmerized!
It looked nothing like what he had pictured.

He felt like he had walked into the jungle.
There were big, beautiful trees with running
streams of water rolling off huge rocks, and
the smell of nature was everywhere.

Frizzle suddenly heard a whistling sound
getting closer and closer,
and he saw the Zoo Train approaching.

The conductor stopped and asked him
if he wanted to climb aboard and
take a tour of the Zoo.
Frizzle explained that he was waiting for
Mr. Owl, but they'd definitely take
the Train Tour later.

Frizzle couldn't wait for Mr. Owl to get there!

He loved this new Zoo already!!!

Because neither Frizzle, nor Mr. Owl, knew their way around the Zoo, they planned on meeting directly inside the entrance. Fortunately for Frizzle, there was a bench there for him to sit and wait.
After all, Mr. Owl wouldn't be there for another thirty minutes.

Frizzle climbed on the bench, realizing that getting up so early had caught up with him. He felt very tired and thought he'd just close his eyes for a couple minutes as he heard the faint whistle of the train again....

11.

Frizzle's Funky Day at the ZOO

As the train came into view,
Frizzle heard loud, uncontrollable laughter.
To his surprise, the laughter was coming from
an elephant passenger and a giraffe that was
driving the train!

Frizzle began smiling,
realizing that he'd never seen animals this
happy or, for that matter, riding on a train!
He had also never seen
animals that looked like THIS!!!

The animals invited Frizzle to climb aboard.

Unable to contain his excitement,
he ran to the train as fast as he could,
and it began its tour of the
Happy Town Zoo and Gardens.

The train started along the jungle-like path,
and as the first exhibit area appeared,
Frizzle realized
there were no glass enclosures.
There were no fences or walls.
The gorillas were running free.
They were laughing and playing and looked
nothing like the gorillas that Frizzle
normally saw at the zoo!

As the train continued on, Frizzle saw lions and hippos playing together in another area. Not only were they playing together, but they too, were bright and colorful—certainly not what Frizzle was used to. And again, there were no fences and no enclosures, and not one animal was trying to get away!

What was going on?

Whatever it was, Frizzle loved it!

Elephants were playing with jaguars.

A baby kangaroo was getting a piggy back ride from a giraffe, and the mommy kangaroo was jumping around with the ball.

Monkeys were teaching penguins to throw
Frisbees, and polar bears were hula hooping.
And did I mention the bright colors
of the animals?

Frizzle had never seen a pink polar bear with
purple hearts all over it!

25.

Frizzle's Funky Day at the ZOO

There was an awesome atmosphere
at this Zoo!

The animals were so happy,
and it warmed Frizzle's heart!

He spotted one of the Zoo Keepers
as the train was approaching an area where
the zebras and tigers were playing.

He immediately ran up to her and asked,
"Miss Patty," (seeing her nametag),
"What in the world is going on at the
Happy Town Zoo and Gardens?
I've never seen anything like it....
I love this place!
Everyone's so happy and carefree here!
There's so much LOVE everywhere!
I don't think I ever want to leave!"

29.

"Whoa, whoa, slow down....
First of all, what's your name?"
asked Miss Patty.

"I'm sorry," said Frizzle. "My name is Frizzle."

Miss Patty said, "Hi Frizzle, it's very nice to
meet you."

"It's very nice to meet you too!" said Frizzle.

"So, you like our Happy Town Zoo
and Gardens, huh?"
asked Miss Patty.

"I love it!!!"
exclaimed Frizzle.

"Yes, Frizzle, we think this place is
pretty special too!" said Miss Patty.

"It's cool how all the animals are so happy. And they're not the colors they're supposed to be. And they all play together. They don't seem to realize that certain kinds of animals don't typically play with other kinds of animals," explained Frizzle.

"So Frizzle, who says that animals are only supposed to be one color or another? And who says that certain animals don't really play with other animals? And who says that because you're this kind of animal or person, you can't do this, or you can't do that?"
asked Miss Patty.

"Well, I don't really know who made those rules, Miss Patty, or even if they are rules. I just know that sometimes it seems that way, or I hear people say things like that," said Frizzle.

"I heard a boy arguing with his sister as I was walking into the Zoo, saying that she shouldn't like football because she's a girl. That she should only like dolls and not sports. Why would he say that, Miss Patty?" asked Frizzle.

"Well, like you said, he probably hears things like that," explained Miss Patty.

"Here at Happy Town Zoo and Gardens, we do things differently. Our residents can look however they want to look. They can have their fur any color they want. They can play with whoever they want, and they can play whatever they want as long as it's safe. And you know what Frizzle, they love it here! We don't have to keep them enclosed in cages or anything else, because they don't want to leave."

"We allow them to be themselves!"

35.

Frizzle's Funky Day at the ZOO

"Wow! I wish the whole world would be like the Happy Town Zoo and Gardens!!!" exclaimed Frizzle.

"Me too!" said Miss Patty.

"Frizzle, Frizzle, wake up Frizzle....
Frizzle, wake up Frizzle...,"
said Mr. Owl.

"Huh, Huh, oh.... Hi, Mr. Owl! I'm sorry, I must have fallen asleep while I was waiting for you. When did you get here?" exclaimed Frizzle.

"Just a couple minutes ago. I'm so excited to see the Zoo. You haven't gone in yet have you?" asked Mr. Owl.

"Umm—" realizing he had just woken out of a dream. "No, no, I haven't gone in. I was waiting for you," said Frizzle, hesitantly.

"Great! Let's go!"

As Frizzle and Mr. Owl began walking
the path of the Zoo,
the train once again came into sight.
The conductor called out to Frizzle, saying,
"Is this the Mr. Owl you were waiting for?"

"Yes, it is," said Frizzle, still slightly dazed
due to the difference between the passengers
in this train and the train in his dream.

Frizzle and Mr. Owl climbed aboard
and began the Train Tour of the
Happy Town Zoo and Gardens.

41.

The train proceeded along the path,
and it was, no doubt, beautiful!
The train stopped every so often
to let the Zoo guests get out and
get close up views of the animals.

Various animals grazed in the grass
and lay on the rocks. They occasionally played
with the other animals in their enclosures.

Zoo guests were allowed to feed the giraffes which Frizzle really enjoyed.

Throughout the afternoon, Mr. Owl and Frizzle saw every resident of the Zoo. They learned many different facts and habits about each one.

45.

Frizzle's Funky Day at the Zoo

As the day wound down, it was time for
Frizzle and Mr. Owl to head home.
They had been at the Zoo for hours.

"Well Frizzle, did you enjoy the Happy Town
Zoo and Gardens?" asked Mr. Owl.

"Yes!" said Frizzle. "I loved it!"

"We certainly saw a lot of different animals
and learned a lot of facts about each
of them," said Mr. Owl.

"We sure did," said Frizzle.

46.

47.

When they returned to Mr. Owl's tree,
Mr. Owl, being the wise old
owl that he is and always trying to teach
something, said, "So Frizzle, what was your
favorite animal, and what was the most
interesting fact you learned today?"

"Hmmm," said Frizzle. "My favorite animal was
the pink polar bear with purple hearts.
The most interesting fact I learned was that
we are all much happier when we're allowed to
be who we want to be and not what others
want us to be!"

"Frizzle, may I ask what in the world you are talking about?"

"Just trust me on this one, Mr. Owl, just trust me!"

Frizzle's Kids ZOO ANIMALS

Frizzle thanks his many friends who sent in drawings of Funky zoo animals.

Alexander

Esme

Alexis

AnnaBella

Frizzle's Kids
ZOO ANIMALS

Allison

Braeden

Bailee

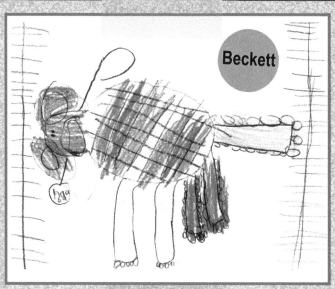

Beckett

Frizzle's Kids
ZOO ANIMALS

Charlie

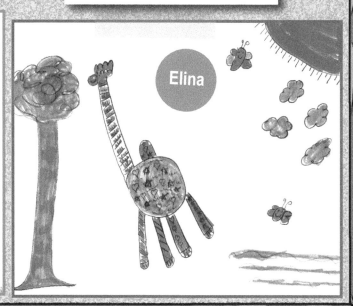

Elina

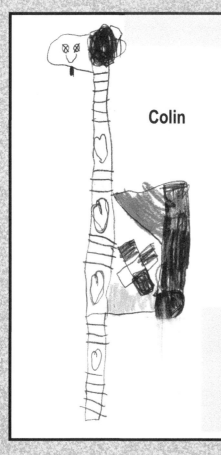

Colin

Connor

Easton

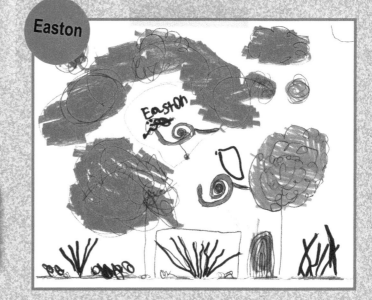

Frizzle's Kids
ZOO ANIMALS

54.

Ramona and London

Harper

Holly

Jaime

Lucy

Pecoce

Patrick

A long neck Zedra

Rory

Frizzle's Kids
ZOO ANIMALS

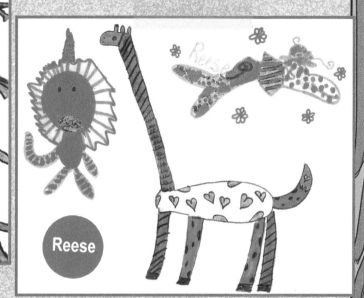

Peyton

Reese

Phoebe

A happy tree

Bloby

rain-bow flower

Frizzle's Kids
ZOO ANIMALS

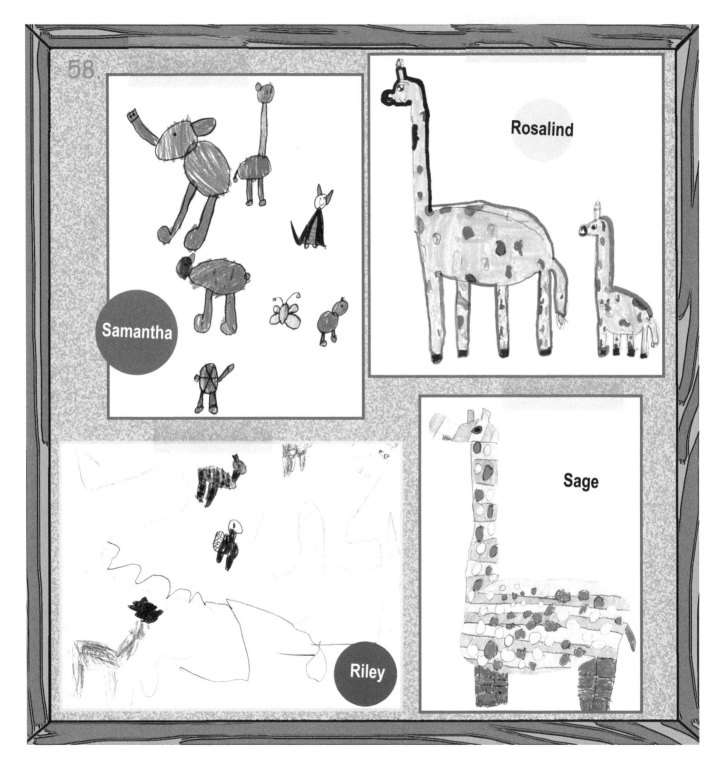

58.

Samantha

Rosalind

Riley

Sage

Sidney

Weston

Sophia

Frizzle's Kids
ZOO ANIMALS

"THANK YOU

Terri Gerrell and Andie Jackson,
for taking what I do and finding a way
to bring it all together and make it better!"

Rhonda Goodall

Rhonda Goodall, an Award-Winning Author and Illustrator of Children's Books, is a wife and Mother of five. She lives in Ponte Vedra Beach, Florida with her husband, Doug, three of their boys, and their dog, Ollie.

Rhonda has spent the majority of her life working with children. She has an incredibly strong passion for molding every child's world into a safe place of happiness, love and kindness. This message is conveyed in the books she writes, as well as every character she introduces. Children immediately fall in love with these unique and fun characters and don't realize that they are learning loving life lessons from each and every one.

You can find Rhonda's books at www.SYPPublishing.com, Amazon.com, Barnes and Noble and various book stores.

Follow her on Facebook: @FrizzleBooks and @RhondaGoodallBooks

Follow her on Instagram at: RhondaGoodall_ and at FrizzleBooks

Follow her on Twitter at: RhondaGoodall_

Books by Rhonda Goodall

Frizzle & Friends Series

Frizzle

Frizzle's Holiday Treasures
FAPA Bronze Medal Presidential Award Winner

Frizzle's Rainbow in the Clouds
FAPA Silver Medal Presidential Award Winner

Frizzle's Funky Day at the Zoo

Where'd Grandma Go...

My Pancreas Needs Glasses
FAPA Silver Medal Presidential Award Winner

COMING SOON!

Frizzle Meets Frazzle

CPSIA information can be obtained
at www.ICGtesting.com
Printed in the USA
LVHW021032301021
701904LV00004B/59